For Charlie Patterson,
who sealed the deal

Who left the beautiful angel on Mandie's doorstep?

"WHAT IN THE WORLD?" she murmured as she bent to look. There was a package wrapped up in brown paper sitting by the back door! "That wasn't there when I came out." She carefully picked it up and glanced at it in the lanternlight. It was not very heavy. "Where did this come from?"

Mandie opened the back door, stepped inside, put out the lantern, and hung it on its peg. Then she turned back to inspect the package before she even removed her coat and tam. Taking it to the table, she laid it down and turned it over.

Miss Amanda Shaw was scribbled in big letters on the brown wrapping paper.

"What is it?" Mandie whispered as she removed the paper. She gasped with glee as she found an angel Christmas ornament. It was old but it was beautiful.

"Oh, how wonderful!" she said as she inspected it. A note underneath was addressed to her.

Miss Amanda Shaw, I know how you love mysteries and I know you can keep a secret. Please keep this a secret just between you and me. I would be most grateful if you would take this to Miss Abigail's when you decorate her tree and put it on top for me, without saying a word to anyone. Thank you for keeping our secret.

Don't miss any of Mandie Shaw's
page-turning mysteries!

And look for the next book, coming soon!

SPECIAL EDITION

Merry Christmas from Mandie

Lois Gladys Leppard

BANTAM BOOKS
NEW YORK • TORONTO • LONDON • SYDNEY • AUCKLAND

RL 2.6, ages 7–10
MERRY CHRISTMAS FROM MANDIE
A Bantam Skylark Book / October 2000

A Special Invitation

"GUESS WHAT?" Mandie Shaw called out as she ran up the lane. Her good friend Joe Woodard was waiting for her on the main road.

"What?" Joe asked as he reached to take her books.

Mandie handed them over. "Miss Abigail is going to have a huge Christmas tree and we are all invited to decorate it," she told him. They began the walk down the road to the schoolhouse. Miss Abigail lived in the finest house in Swain County, North Carolina. "And she has piles of Christmas decorations in her attic and we can go up there and choose what we want to use. Isn't that exciting?"

Joe smiled down at Mandie. "I'd say it's *interesting*. As long as Miss Abigail has been living here in Charley Gap, she has never had a Christmas tree."

"She's doing this for Faith," Mandie declared.

Faith Winters and her grandmother, Mrs. Chapman, had come to Charley Gap in the western North Carolina mountains earlier that fall and had moved into the ramshackle old Conley place. Mr. Conley had moved away years before, and the local people were surprised to learn that he had gone to Missouri to live with Faith's family, who were his relatives. Upon his death his house in North Carolina had become the property of Faith and her grandmother. And after Faith's parents were killed in a fire that destroyed their home in Missouri, she and her grandmother had come to live in it. Now she and Mandie were good friends.

Miss Abigail had given Faith a home while Faith's grandmother, the girl's only living relative, went to New York for medical treatment. "Faith's grandmother may not be back in time for Christmas," Mandie said. "She wrote Faith a letter and said the doctors are still treating those scars on her face." Mrs. Chapman had been badly burned in the fire.

"Yes, her doctor wrote my dad a letter. He thinks he might be able to help her enough that she won't be shy about being seen in public," Joe replied.

"Oh, that would be wonderful!" Mandie exclaimed. "You know, when I first saw her face it hurt me inside. It looked so terrible I just had to try real hard to keep from crying in front of her." She blinked her blue eyes as she felt the threat of tears.

"Well, we've got her house in top shape. Everything is repaired," Joe said. "Now we have to refurnish the inside."

"Joe, I just can't imagine our house burning up along with everything in it," Mandie said. "And from what I can gather, they must have had an awfully beautiful home in Missouri. Now they have to live in Mr. Conley's old place."

"If Mr. Conley were still living, he'd never recognize his house now," Joe said. "It's lucky for Faith and her grandmother that they inherited the place right at the time they needed a home."

Mandie looked up at Joe. "Do you think Miss Abigail will let all of us go hunt for a Christmas tree?" she asked. "I know she's got people working there for her who could do it, but do you think maybe she'll let us do it instead?"

"She might. Who did Miss Abigail say she was going to invite?" he asked.

"All of us, all of the pupils at our school," Mandie said.

"There are sixteen of us, Mandie," Joe reminded her. "Do you think Miss Abigail will really have all those people over to decorate just one Christmas tree?"

Mandie stopped in the middle of the road, stomped her foot, and looked up at Joe. "Joe Woodard, I said she is going to ask all of us, which, in my opinion, means all sixteen pupils," she said firmly.

"All right, all right, let's go. We're going to be late for school," Joe said with a smile as he turned to go.

Mandie quickly caught up with him. "I know sixteen people are going to be a crowd to get into her attic, but she has a big house, so it'll hold them all," she told him.

"How did you find out about this?" Joe asked, walking faster as the schoolhouse came within sight.

"She and Faith brought Windy home last night," Mandie explained.

"Your cat? What was it doing over at Miss Abigail's house?" Joe asked.

"I don't know," Mandie answered, short of breath. Her nine-year-old legs had a hard time keeping up with Joe's eleven-year-old ones. They turned down the lane to the log schoolhouse. "I suppose Windy went off and got lost and happened to find her way to Miss Abigail's."

They stepped up onto the porch and entered the front door of the one-room schoolhouse. Mr. Tallant was at his desk, but they were the first pupils to arrive. Stopping at the pegs near the door, they removed their coats and hats and hung them up.

"Good morning. Y'all are here bright and early," the schoolmaster greeted them as he looked up from his paperwork.

"Yes, sir. Joe practically ran all the way, afraid that we'd be late," Mandie said as she went to her desk, where Joe deposited her books.

"I would hate to be late," Joe told her with a big smile. Then he added, "I was thinking about all those ornaments you said Miss Abigail has in her attic. They must be awfully old."

"Maybe they're not too old to use," Mandie replied, sitting down at her desk.

"If they are, we could make some new ones," Joe suggested.

"Make new ones? That would be a job, with the huge tree she is planning to have. She said it would be tall enough to touch the ceiling," Mandie said.

"With sixteen of us working on them, it wouldn't take long," Joe said. "The boys could carve the ornaments, and the girls could paint them and add ribbons."

Mr. Tallant spoke from his desk. "Joe, I think you have a very good idea. We need to have a class on woodworking, since the girls are attending those needlework sessions Miss Abigail is hosting. We'll discuss it in class today."

"Yes, sir," Joe said, looking pleased.

"We may not need new ornaments, Mr. Tallant," Mandie spoke up. "Miss Abigail said she has piles of them in her attic." She paused. "But it would be nice if each one of us took one ornament to give her."

"Yes, I'm sure she would appreciate that. We'll

see what we can work out," the schoolmaster promised.

As the other pupils began arriving and going to their desks, Mandie was eager to share the news of Miss Abigail's invitation. However, she knew that Faith was going to ask everyone.

After Mr. Tallant called the roll, he motioned to Faith to come forward. "Faith has a message for all of you from Miss Abigail," he said, smiling.

Faith, still shy with her new friends, walked quickly up front. "Miss Abigail would like for me to extend an invitation to all of you to come to her house and help decorate the Christmas tree two weeks from Saturday at six o' clock," she said in a low voice. She started to hurry back to her desk when several pupils asked questions.

"Are our parents invited, too?" a girl named Dorothy asked.

"Where is she going to get the tree?" a boy named Fred asked.

"But Miss Abigail never has a Christmas tree," Esther spoke up.

Mr. Tallant tapped lightly on his desk. "Now I know you all have lots of questions, but please wait and ask them at recess. We need to get our lessons under way. And I would like to talk to the boys about a woodworking class."

During lessons, Mandie thought about all those Christmas tree ornaments that Miss Abigail had in her attic. She wondered why the lady had such decorations if she never put up a Christmas tree. Everybody in Charley Gap had a Christmas tree, no matter how poor. And Miss Abigail certainly wasn't poor. She had built the biggest and most expensive house in the neighborhood and had furnished it with beautiful and costly belongings.

"It's a mystery," Mandie murmured to herself, and then quickly looked around the room as she realized she had spoken aloud. But no one seemed to have noticed.

Then she thought about the Christmas tree she and her father would get from the woods. Christmas was coming so quickly! She needed to start making presents for her family and also for her friends. She wanted to give everybody something, but what? She had no money. She would have to think of things she could make.

When recess finally came, Mandie wanted to

ask Faith some questions. But everyone else in the class had the same idea.

"Are we supposed to bring anything?"

"What time are we expected?"

"Why is Miss Abigail having a tree this year?"

Mandie and Joe sat together in a back corner of the schoolroom and listened; the weather was too cold to eat outside.

Mandie turned to Joe. "It is strange that Miss Abigail is putting up a Christmas tree this year when she's never had one before."

"But she lives alone, and like you said, now that Faith is there, she's probably doing this for her," Joe reminded her. He hurriedly ate his sweet roll.

"Then why does she have ornaments in the attic?" Mandie asked, quickly swallowing the last bite of her biscuit with ham.

"Well, she must have had a tree sometime, back wherever she came from," Joe said.

"I think there's something mysterious about it all," Mandie replied.

Joe frowned. "Mandie Shaw, why do you always try to make a mystery out of everything?"

Mandie frowned back at him. "Not everything, Joe. Just certain things that puzzle me. Like this Christmas tree!"

At that moment Esther came over to sit down by Mandie. "Imagine, Miss Abigail putting up a Christmas tree!" she said.

"That's what you normally do at Christmastime," Joe said.

"But Miss Abigail is not normal. She has never had a tree since she moved here," Esther reminded him.

"You know, this conversation is just going around in circles," Joe said, frowning again. "Let's not make a mountain out of a molehill."

Irene, Mandie's older sister, came over to join them. "I know what y'all are talking about, because everyone is talking about the same thing," she told them. She pushed back her long dark hair. "And I don't think it's worth all that talk."

Joe grinned. "For once, Irene, you and I agree."

"I'm not sure I want to agree with you, because you never agree with me," Irene told him as she sat down on the end of the next bench.

"Y'all are planning to go to Miss Abigail's,

aren't you?" Esther asked, looking from Joe to Irene.

Joe shrugged. "I suppose so," he said.

"I'm not sure. It depends on what else is going on at that time," Irene replied.

Mandie looked curiously at her sister. "What do you mean by that? What else are you talking about?"

Irene cleared her throat. "Oh, you know, first one thing and then another." She looked across the room.

"You want to wait and see if Tommy Lester is coming?" Mandie guessed. Irene liked Tommy. Mandie knew he didn't like parties, so he might not go.

"Now I didn't mention his name, Mandie," Irene quickly told her.

At that moment the bell rang and everyone hurried back to their desks. Mandie glanced across the room at her sister and wondered whether she would really give up the opportunity to help decorate Miss Abigail's tree just because of Tommy Lester.

When school let out for the day, Mandie noticed Tommy Lester was the first one out the door and Irene was right behind him.

"Guess your sister is not going to walk home with us today," Joe remarked as they took their coats down from the pegs.

"Guess not," Mandie agreed and turned to Faith behind her. "But I hope you are, Faith."

"Yes, as far as the usual crossroad," Faith replied.

"Have you seen the ornaments that Miss Abigail has in the attic?" Mandie asked Faith as the three walked down the road together.

"No, I haven't," Faith said, turning her coat collar up to buffer the wind.

"Does Miss Abigail have a whole lot of stuff up there?" Mandie wanted to know next. She pushed her hands deep into her coat pockets to keep them warm even though she was wearing gloves.

"I don't know, Mandie. I've never *been* in Miss Abigail's attic," Faith replied. "She keeps it locked," she added.

"Locked?" Mandie repeated in surprise.

"Yes, Miss Dicey said Miss Abigail has always kept her attic locked. Even Miss Dicey has never been in it," Faith explained. Miss Dicey was Miss Abigail's housekeeper.

"I wonder why?" Mandie asked, puzzled.

"She probably keeps it locked to safeguard whatever she has in it," Joe remarked with a frown.

"But nobody in Charley Gap locks anything," Mandie protested.

"She does. She even locks her doors when she leaves the house," Faith told them.

"Well she does have some expensive furnishings, not like the usual household here in the country," Joe reminded them. Then, turning to grin down at Mandie he added, "Of course, you are only nine years old. You may not be old enough to realize that."

"Oh, Joe Woodard, you are only eleven yourself, which is not much more than nine. You don't know everything either," Mandie told him.

Faith looked at both of them, smiled, and said, "Neither of you has ever lived in a city like I have. Let me tell you, everybody in the city locks their doors."

"They do?" Mandie asked.

"Yes. There are so many people in the city, you

can't know everybody like you do here. You don't know who might not be honest," Faith explained. "Anyhow, I like the country here better than the city."

"Do you know if Miss Abigail ever lived in a city?" Mandie asked.

"I have no idea," Faith said, shaking her head. "She has never mentioned anything to me about where she has lived."

Mandie decided there must be lots of mysteries surrounding Miss Abigail. She wanted to solve some of them.

Faith left them at the crossroad and went on down the road toward Miss Abigail's house. Mandie and Joe continued on their way. When they reached the lane to Mandie's house, Joe gave Mandie her books, said goodbye, and turned to go back down the road to his house.

Mandie rushed down the lane and saw her father working on the split-rail fence he was putting around the boundary of their property. Her cat, Windy, came to greet her. She picked up Windy and stopped to speak to her father.

"We were talking about Miss Abigail at school after Faith invited everyone to come decorate the

Christmas tree," Mandie told Mr. Shaw. "Daddy, where did Miss Abigail come from? How long has she been living here?"

Jim Shaw straightened up from his work. "Now, let me see, my little blue-eyes, I believe Miss Abigail moved here around about the time you were still a baby, but I've never known where she came from. No one else does either, that I know of."

"Oh, shucks! I figured you knew everything, Daddy," Mandie said with a smile, cuddling Windy in one arm and holding her books in the other.

"That's impossible," he said, smiling back at her. "But now, with someone like you, why, you might just solve that mystery one day."

"I'm thinking about it," Mandie said. "Maybe I can."

2

Plans

MANDIE WENT IN the back door of the house, which opened directly into the kitchen. Her mother was sitting by the huge iron cook-stove, knitting.

"Get your homework done, then you can set the table for me. I've got everything waiting on top of the stove," Mrs. Shaw greeted her as she glanced up from wrapping the yarn around the needles.

"Yes, ma'am," Mandie replied. She stooped to deposit her kitten on the floor, laid her books on a chair, and began unbuttoning her coat. The heat from the stove felt good after the long cold walk from the schoolhouse. She removed her coat and gloves and went to hold her hands over the burners to warm them.

"I don't have much homework, just a few

arithmetic problems," Mandie said. She watched the yarn flying back and forth on the knitting needles. "Mama, I need to make some presents for my friends," she said. "And I don't know what."

"Well, if you get busy with things right now, you should be able to finish quite a few presents before Christmas," her mother said. "You could embroider some handkerchiefs made out of that piece of white cotton left over from the new sheets. You could draw some pictures for some of your friends. You are good at that. You could even make a corncob doll, maybe for Faith."

"Those all seem like good ideas," Mandie agreed, turning to pick up her books and her coat. "But, goodness, Mama, I'm not very fast. It would take forever to make all *that*."

Mrs. Shaw looked up at her. "Just how many people are you planning on giving presents to?"

Mandie thought for a moment. "You, Daddy, and Irene, of course. And there's Faith and Joe. They're both important. Dr. and Mrs. Woodard. And I suppose Esther. And I always give Mr. Tallant something, and then we are going to Miss Abigail's in two weeks and I should have a present ready to put under her tree then. Whew! Christmas is just getting here too fast this year."

"Don't forget, you'll have almost two weeks out of school before Christmas. I'll see what I can do to help you," Mrs. Shaw told her.

"You will? Thank you, Mama," Mandie said gratefully. "I'll hurry and hang my things up and get my homework done." She hung her coat and tam on the pegs by the parlor door and stuffed her gloves in the pockets. Taking her books, she went to sit by the crackling fire in the fireplace. Windy followed her and curled up on the warm hearth.

"Now, let me see. I need to do some arithmetic for myself," Mandie murmured as she flipped to a clean sheet in her tablet and began scribbling. "It's about four weeks till Christmas. And I need to make at least ten presents—say, twelve presents to be safe. That means I will have to get these done at three presents per week." She sat back and twirled the pencil in her hand. "Now I need to decide what I am going to make and what I am going to give everybody." She hummed under her breath.

Windy opened one eye and looked up at her mistress. She meowed softly and went back to sleep.

Mandie bent down from her chair to stroke the kitten's head. "How lucky you are to be a cat, Windy. You don't have to go through all this," she told her. "I have to get something for you, too, although you probably won't even know it's Christmas when it comes. Still, I want you to be a good cat and celebrate Jesus's birthday with me."

The front door suddenly flew open and Irene rushed into the room, throwing her books on a chair and hanging her coat and tam on the pegs.

"Do you have homework?" Mandie asked.

"I've already done it. Tommy and I stopped at that log bench down in the curve and did it. We didn't have much," Irene told her. She came to stand before the fire and warm her hands. "You doing yours?"

"I am in a minute," Mandie replied, looking down at her list. "I'm trying to figure out what I will give everybody for Christmas. I'll have to make everything."

"I wouldn't go to all that trouble," Irene said,

with a shrug. "Just wrap up some of Mama's jelly or something."

"Irene, that would take too much jelly. I have ten people on my list," Mandie said.

"Well, you can be sure I'm not giving that many presents," Irene said, turning to face her sister and letting the heat warm her back.

"The main one to get ready right now is something for Miss Abigail, so we can take it when we decorate the tree," Mandie said, twirling her pencil.

"I'll just ask Mama if I can take her a jar of that blackberry jam we made last summer. After all, I did help pick the blackberries," Irene told her.

"That would be nice," Mandie agreed, frowning as she thought. Then she added with a smile, "I know what I'll give her. I'll get Daddy to help me make her a feather duster like the one he made for Mama."

"She probably has a feather duster. In fact, she probably has everything," Irene reminded her.

"Well, it wouldn't hurt to have an extra duster," Mandie replied. "Besides, I've got so many gifts to make I have to make quick decisions about what they will be, and a feather duster sounds like something Miss Abigail could use," Mandie said. She quickly scribbled on the sheet of paper: *Miss Abigail, a feather duster.* Then, looking up at her sister, she asked, "What are you going to give Mama and Daddy?"

"Oh, goodness, who ever started this business of giving presents at Christmas, anyhow?" Irene said with a loud sigh.

"Irene, you know the answer to that," Mandie said with a frown. "The three wise men."

"What are *you* going to give Mama and Daddy?" Irene asked.

"Those handkerchiefs I've been making at Miss Abigail's needlework classes. They don't know about them. Mama thinks we are only doing table scarves and doilies," Mandie said. "We're going to start on some fancy pillows next week. Why don't you come and do some of those?"

"Mandie, I can't do that kind of work," Irene protested. "It's too hard."

Mandie thought for a moment. "All right, then," she said. "I'll make the pillows for their chairs, and you can have the handkerchiefs I've been working on."

"Really?" Irene asked.

Mandie nodded. "Only you will have to finish the edges if I have to start on the pillows. I won't have time to do it all."

"All right," Irene said. "Thanks."

"If you will help me with the dusters, we can give one together to Miss Abigail and one to Dr. and Mrs. Woodard," Mandie said hopefully.

"Oh, well, I suppose I could, if Daddy will show us how," Irene reluctantly agreed.

"Thanks," Mandie said with a big smile. "Now I have to get my homework done so I can set the table for supper." She opened her arithmetic book.

"I'll set the table," Irene offered as she started toward the kitchen door.

Mandie looked up in surprise. Irene never volunteered to do any chore. "You will?" she asked.

Irene looked back and said with a shrug, "Well, you're going to help me out with the Christmas presents, so I guess I can set the table." She went through the doorway and closed the door behind her.

Mandie sat there with a big smile. Her sister could be nice if she wanted to.

Later, as they sat around the supper table, the discussion was about Christmas.

"When are we going to get our tree and put it up, Daddy?" Mandie asked, laying down her fork.

"Why don't we find the tree on Sunday, after Miss Abigail puts hers up on Saturday. We can put ours up Monday night and you girls can invite all your friends," Mr. Shaw said, his blue eyes smiling at Mandie.

Mandie and Irene looked at each other at that news.

"We think you are both old enough now to have a little Christmas tree–decorating party, especially since Miss Abigail seems to think you're old enough to attend one," Mrs. Shaw told the girls.

"Oh, thank you, Mama, Daddy," Mandie said, pushing back wisps of blond hair from her face and straightening up in her chair.

"Do we get to invite anyone we want to?" Irene asked, looking from her mother to her father.

"Well, yes, I suppose so," Mr. Shaw replied, sipping his cup of coffee.

Mrs. Shaw looked sternly at Irene. "Yes, you may invite Tommy Lester, if that's who you are thinking of."

"Yes, Mama. Thank you, Mama," Irene said. She grinned at Mandie, who smiled back.

"Daddy, Irene and I want to make feather dusters for Miss Abigail and Dr. and Mrs. Woodard for Christmas. Could you help us, please?" Mandie asked, taking a quick bite of the beans on her plate.

"Feather dusters? Now that's a right bright idea," Mr. Shaw said, setting down his coffee cup. "Sure, I'll help you girls, but now if you want the presents to be from you two, then you are going to have to do most of the work. I still have some turkey feathers in the attic that we can use, and we'll need to whittle the handles out and paint them. And I'll have to see if I have enough twine to assemble them."

"We'll need to take Miss Abigail's with us when we go to her house to decorate her tree. Do you think we can make one that fast?" Mandie asked.

"With three of us working on one duster, I don't see why not," Mr. Shaw replied. "But we might as well make both of them at the same time. That will save going through the whole process twice."

"All right," Mandie said and looking at her sister, she asked, "Would you make one and I'll make the other one?"

"I suppose so, but Daddy, you're going to have to help me. I have no idea how you make a duster," Irene said with a loud sigh.

"Of course, dear, but when we get finished I'm sure you will be an expert. You may even want to make more for other people's presents," Mr. Shaw told her.

"That would be a good present for some of our friends," Mrs. Shaw agreed.

Mandie suddenly remembered Mrs. Chapman, Faith's grandmother. "What if Mrs. Chapman gets back in time for Christmas?" she asked, looking at her mother. "Shouldn't we go ahead and make something for her, just in case?"

"Of course," Mrs. Shaw replied, laying down her fork. "All of us women are refurnishing the curtains, counterpanes, and such in her house to have it ready for her return. Maybe you girls want to help."

"Oh, no, not that kind of work," Irene protested. *"I'll* help paint."

"Paint?" Mr. Shaw asked. "Well, all right, Irene. We have to get the inside painted and dried before the ladies can put the new furnishings in."

"Me too, Daddy?" Mandie asked. "I'd love to paint."

"Mandie, you're not going to have time to make all those presents you are planning to give, much less help paint," Irene reminded her.

"Well . . . ," Mandie said slowly. "Maybe I could help just a little bit." She looked at her father and then at her mother. Painting was always fun.

"We'll see," Mr. Shaw said, drinking his coffee.

"Just remember you have to have those presents finished in time for Christmas," Mrs. Shaw reminded her.

"Yes, ma'am," Mandie agreed. She knew she couldn't do two things at one time, and it was either make the presents or help paint. She'd have to settle for making presents. Maybe she could think of some kind of present that would require painting!

"Don't look so glum. You can't do everything," her father said as he smiled across the table. "And the boys are going to help us, so we'll have plenty of help."

"The boys?" Mandie said suddenly. "Oh, the boys are going to make new ornaments for Miss Abigail's tree, I think. Joe suggested we each take one to her when we visit that night. And they'll have to be painted." She grinned at her father.

"So you'll be able to mess in that paint after all," Mr. Shaw teased her.

"That's a nice idea, taking new ornaments to Miss Abigail," Mrs. Shaw remarked. "Whatever she has in her attic must be terribly old. She's never had a tree up during all the years she's lived here."

"That's what everyone has been saying, Mama," Mandie said. "Where did Miss Abigail come from?"

"I don't believe anyone knows for sure," she said. "Seems like it must have been some big city somewhere, because of all the expensive furnishings she brought for her house here."

"Oh, shucks!" Mandie said with a loud sigh. "No one knows anything about Miss Abigail. I was hoping you did. Everyone at school is talking like lightning because she is putting up a tree for the first time. And we can't wait to get in her attic. There's no telling what she has in there. Faith says she keeps it locked and even Miss Dicey has never been in it."

"No one has," Irene said.

"Have you ever been in Miss Abigail's attic, Mama?" Mandie asked.

Mrs. Shaw frowned. "Of course not. Why would I be going into Miss Abigail's attic?"

"I just thought maybe she might have some things stored away up there and might have shown them to you," Mandie explained.

"No, I have never been in her attic and don't have any idea I ever will," Mrs. Shaw replied. "Now let's get finished with our supper so we can clean up the kitchen for the night." She picked up her fork and began eating the remainder of the food on her plate.

"Yes, ma'am," Mandie said, taking a big bite out of her biscuit.

"We'll begin on those dusters after you girls come home from school tomorrow," Mr. Shaw told them.

"Yes, sir," Mandie said with a smile.

"Yes, let's get those things done and over with," Irene agreed.

As Mandie chewed, she imagined an attic crammed full of boxes and furniture, with drawers full of old possessions. Miss Abigail must have brought a lot of stuff with her when she came to live at Charley Gap. She could hardly wait to see everything.

3

A Secret

THE NEXT AFTERNOON Mandie and Irene began work on the two feather dusters. Mr. Shaw whittled the handles out of pieces of firewood stacked in the barn and had them watch.

"I'll do this part because I don't trust you two with a knife," he told the girls as he shaved slivers off the wood to get it into shape. "You see, the wood has to be trimmed down small enough to hold in your hand and then smoothed off to get rid of any splinters."

"Then what do we do, Daddy?" Mandie asked, tiptoeing in close to see every stroke.

"Well, next, the handle needs to be painted and dried," he replied.

"And that's what I get to do," Irene remarked from her perch on a stack of hay nearby.

"And then we'll get those turkey feathers out of the storage bin in the attic, and I'll show you how to attach them to the handle," Mr. Shaw explained.

Mandie looked at her sister. "Irene, you make one and I'll make the other. That way we both get to paint."

Irene shrugged. "Well, all right," she said. "But don't forget, you said we would put both our names on both dusters, one to the Woodards and one to Miss Abigail."

"We will," Mandie promised. "I would just like to learn how to make a whole duster."

"I believe I have one handle about finished," Mr. Shaw said, surveying the stick of wood in his hand. "Now I'll just bore a small hole through the handle so we can insert a cord to hang it with." As the girls watched he quickly finished the handle and held it up for them to see.

"All done?" Mandie asked as she looked at the piece of wood.

"As soon as I get the cord over here and attach it, one of you can go ahead and paint the handle," he told them.

"Irene, you go first, if you want to," Mandie offered.

"Thank you, Mandie, I will," Irene replied, smiling at her.

Mr. Shaw took down a ball of twine from a shelf high on the wall of the barn. He cut off a piece and then cut the piece in half as the girls watched.

"Irene, since you are doing the first one, run this cord through the hole in the handle and I'll show you how to tie it so it won't come out," Mr. Shaw said, handing the piece of wood and one piece of the twine to Irene.

Irene poked the cord through the hole and her father tied the two ends into a strong knot, testing it to be sure it wouldn't come apart.

"Now come over here. I've got some paint ready and you can paint this one," Mr. Shaw told Irene, leading the way across the barn to another shelf where an open paint bucket stood. "We'll hang this up so you don't get paint all over yourself. Then we'll leave it hanging until it is dry, which will probably be tomorrow." He hung the piece of wood on a nail near the bucket, then picked up a small paintbrush next to it and handed it to Irene.

Irene looked at the paint in the bucket. "This paint is red. Are we going to paint both dusters red?"

"I thought that would be a nice color, since it's a Christmas present," Mr. Shaw explained.

"Oh, yes, red would be just right," Mandie agreed.

Irene tossed back her hair. "Well, I suppose it will be all right."

"Please be very careful and do not get a drop of that paint on your clothes or we will have your mother to answer to," Mr. Shaw cautioned.

Irene carefully began dipping the brush into the paint and reached up to put the first strokes on the new handle.

"Now we will get the other handle ready for you, Amanda," Mr. Shaw said.

By the time the two handles were painted and hanging up to dry, the afternoon was gone. The girls surveyed their work. "I think Miss Abigail and Mrs. Woodard will both like those red handles," Mandie said. "We can tie a big red ribbon bow on each one."

Irene frowned. "Just where are we going to get the red ribbon?" Irene asked. "We didn't even have money to buy presents."

"There's some ribbon left from last Christmas, if Mama will let us use it," Mandie replied.

"Speaking of your mother, we'd better get back to the house and wash up. She may need some help with supper," Mr. Shaw told the girls.

When they entered the kitchen, Mrs. Shaw already had supper waiting on the cookstove, the table was set, and she was sitting in the chair next to the woodbox, busily knitting.

"Wash up, girls, and we'll eat. Then y'all can do your homework," she told them as she laid down her knitting.

"We don't have any homework, Mama," Mandie told her. "Mr. Tallant said he won't be giving us any more until after Christmas, because he knows we are all busy getting ready for the holiday."

"That's awfully considerate of him. Maybe I can help you girls work on those handkerchiefs you are going to give your friends," Mrs. Shaw told them, going to the stove.

"Thank you, Mama," Mandie said.

"Me too, Mama," Irene added.

As soon as supper was over and the table cleared, Mandie and Irene laid out their needlework. The handkerchiefs Mandie had been making at Miss Abigail's needlework classes were hidden away and were for their parents. So far, the white material had only been cut up into squares.

"Now we'll just roll and whip the edges like this," Mrs. Shaw said as she threaded a needle with white thread and then rolled up the edge of one of the squares with her thumb. She began stitching it down in tiny, almost invisible, stitches.

"You expect me to do that?" Irene asked, blowing out her breath.

"Irene, you are capable of doing more than you give yourself credit for," their mother said. "Here, take this one I've started and I'll guide you through it."

Mrs. Shaw handed the piece of white material with the needle attached to Irene. "Just go real slow and you'll learn how to do this," she encouraged her.

Mandie watched for a moment and then went

to work on the one she was making. She had already learned how to finish the edges. Her cat, Windy, sat beside her, watching the thread. "Windy, don't you dare jump for this thread," Mandie told the yellow cat. She pulled the work closer into her lap. Windy meowed, stretched, and went across the room to jump into the woodbox behind the warm cookstove.

"Mama, do you think Miss Abigail will like the duster?" Mandie asked as she stitched.

"I'm sure she will, especially since you girls made it," Mrs. Shaw replied. "Nearly everything she owns is store-bought. I'd think she'd appreciate something handmade."

"I suppose everything she gives other people for Christmas comes from a store somewhere, too," Mandie said, watching her neat stitches.

"Yes, she goes off over the mountain every year to do her shopping," Mrs. Shaw remarked.

Mandie looked up at her mother. "Where does she go? Are there big stores somewhere across the mountain?"

"There are lots of stores in towns beyond the mountain, Amanda," Mrs. Shaw said. "Someday

I'll take you girls over there." She watched Irene closely. "Don't forget to keep the edge rolled up so you can't see the raggedy threads, Irene."

"Yes, ma'am," Irene replied, without looking up from what she was doing.

"Mama, does Miss Abigail have kinpeople across the mountain? She doesn't have any around here," Mandie said. She looked up for her mother's reaction.

"She might," Mrs. Shaw replied. "Now pay attention to your work there, Amanda, so we can get something done. I can only do one thing at a time, and I have to see that Irene is doing this right if you girls want these finished by Christmas," Mrs. Shaw told her.

Mr. Shaw came into the kitchen, took a cup and saucer from the cabinet, and went to the cookstove. He picked up the steaming percolator and poured hot coffee into his cup.

"Daddy, does Miss Abigail have kinpeople somewhere?" Mandie asked.

Mr. Shaw replied, "I have no idea."

Mrs. Shaw said, "Amanda, are you going to work on these handkerchiefs or not? If you are, then get on with it."

Mandie looked from her mother back to her father, who was silently carrying his cup of coffee back to the parlor, where he had been reading by the fireplace.

Mandie pursed her lips and bent over the handkerchief. Maybe Miss Abigail did have kinpeople over the mountain, since the lady went there at least once a year. When Mandie got a chance, she would ask her. But then, Miss Abigail was so secretive about her own affairs she might not tell her anything.

"Won't hurt to ask anyway," Mandie murmured to herself.

Mrs. Shaw looked sharply at her. Mandie began quickly stitching the handkerchief as she thought about the secrets adults always seemed to have. Then Mandie had a sudden thought. Maybe that was why Miss Abigail had kept her past secret—maybe she had some bad kinpeople somewhere.

Mandie could never give up on a mystery until she had solved it. So later, when everyone was preparing for bed, she asked permission to stay up longer.

"Mama, could I just sit here by the stove and

read a while before I go to bed? I haven't had time to read much lately," Mandie asked as she folded up her needlework.

Mrs. Shaw hesitated for a moment. "I suppose you can stay up a little while, but don't be too late or you won't want to get up in the morning. Tomorrow is a school day, you know." She put their needlework into her large workbasket and took it with her as she started for the parlor.

"I am going to bed. I'm tired and sleepy," Irene said as she hurried from the kitchen.

"I won't stay up long," Mandie promised. She followed her mother into the parlor, where she took a book from the table and told her parents goodnight.

Mandie went back to sit by the cookstove, pushed her chair near the woodbox, propped her feet up, and opened the book. She tried to concentrate on the story but found her mind wandering.

She smiled as she imagined Miss Abigail accepting the duster. And then she frowned as she wondered what was in Miss Abigail's attic that she had always kept locked. She couldn't wait to get inside the place and see for herself just what was there. Squirming around in her chair, she straightened her skirts and suddenly realized there was a button missing from the waistband. Luckily there were two buttons on it, or she might have lost her skirt!

"Now where did it go?" she murmured as she rose and began searching the kitchen floor. There was no sign of it. Losing a button was serious—buttons were hard to get in Charley Gap out in the western North Carolina mountains.

"Oh, shucks!" she whispered. "I must have lost it out in the barn. I'd better go see if I can find it before Mama knows it's missing."

The weather was too cold outside to go out without her coat and tam, so she silently crept through the doorway to the pegs where they hung, got them, and came back into the kitchen to put them on.

Windy immediately began meowing as she watched her mistress. "You can't go now, you hear," Mandie whispered to the yellow cat as she went to get the lantern her father kept hanging by the back door. She quickly lit the wick and slipped outside.

"Br-r-r-r!" She shivered as she practically ran toward the barn.

Once inside the building, she slowed down to inspect every inch of the floor where she had walked that afternoon. She was about to give up when she finally spotted something white shining through the straw. Reaching down to flip away the straw, she smiled as she uncovered the button.

"There you are!" she said to herself. "Thank goodness I found you." She carefully put the button in her coat pocket and turned to go back to the house.

The weather was so cold she didn't waste time. As she stepped up on the porch and rushed to open the back door, she stumbled over something and almost fell.

"What in the world?" she murmured as she bent to look. There was a package wrapped up in brown paper sitting by the back door! "That wasn't there when I came out." She carefully picked it up and glanced at it in the lanternlight.

It was not very heavy. "Where did this come from?"

Mandie opened the back door, stepped inside, put out the lantern, and hung it on its peg. Then she turned back to inspect the package before she even removed her coat and tam. Taking it to the table, she laid it down and turned it over.

Miss Amanda Shaw was scribbled in big letters on the brown wrapping paper.

"What is it?" Mandie whispered as she removed the paper. She gasped with glee as she found an angel Christmas ornament. It was old but it was beautiful.

"Oh, how wonderful!" she said as she inspected it. A note underneath was addressed to her.

Miss Amanda Shaw,

I know how you love mysteries and I know you can keep a secret. Please keep this a secret just between you and me. I would be most grateful if you would take this to Miss Abigail's when you decorate her tree and put it on the top for me,

without saying a word to anyone. Thank you for
keeping our secret.

There was no signature.

"Well, whoever did this must have wanted to stay secretive themselves," Mandie said as she once more examined the angel. Turning it over, she noticed a small chip on one of the angel's wings. At first she thought that she might have chipped it when she ran into the package on the porch, but upon looking closer she could tell it was an old chip that had turned color with age.

Mandie slowly removed her coat and tam as she thought about the strange package. Where did it come from? Someone must have placed it on the porch before she had returned from the barn.

"Now who would want to do such a thing?" she wondered to herself. "I can't think of a single soul. Not only that, the angel is old, so it must belong to someone who has had it for an awfully long time."

She rewrapped the angel and decided to hide it under her bed until the day came to go to Miss Abigail's. The note asked her to keep it a secret, so she couldn't discuss it with anyone, not even Joe. And she always shared secrets with Joe.

She sighed. "Oh, well, I'll tell Joe all about it as soon as I put it on Miss Abigail's tree. And just maybe whoever sent this to me will be there, too, and will let me know who they are. I just can't stop until I find out who did this."

When she went up to her room for the night she silently pushed the package under her bed, looked across the room to be sure her sister was asleep, and then finally climbed into bed herself. But sleep was long coming that night. She had a mystery to think about. . . . And she was determined to solve it.

4

Joe Is Curious

THE NEXT DAY Mandie could think of nothing but the angel. She got up and ate breakfast, but she had little to say as she got ready for school.

"Amanda, are you not feeling well?" Mrs. Shaw asked as they sat at the table.

Mandie shoved her grits around on her plate. She didn't know what to say. She couldn't tell anyone about the angel, but it had her worried. "I'm all right, Mama."

"Then you'd better get a move on and finish your breakfast," Mrs. Shaw told her. "I suppose you stayed up too late last night."

"Remember, early to bed, early to rise, makes a man healthy, wealthy, and wise," her father reminded her across the table.

Before Mandie could reply, Irene spoke up. "I

don't believe in that old saying," she argued. "I go to bed early most of the time and I'm not wealthy."

"Oh, but you're not old enough yet to become wealthy. Just be patient," her father said.

"Well, at least I'm healthy," Mandie remarked, quickly eating the last of the food on her plate. "However, sometimes I wonder if I'm wise." She frowned as she looked at her father.

"I would say you're both wise for your age," Mr. Shaw said. "You've both done well in school so far, and that's what builds the foundation for your future."

"I just wish the future would hurry up and get here. I'm not too crazy about school," Irene remarked, draining the last sip of coffee from her cup.

"You can't just reach out and get whatever you want in life, Irene," Mr. Shaw reminded her. "You have to work up to it, keep your goal in your mind."

"My goal right now is to get to school on time," Mandie said, rising from the table. Everyone else rose, too.

Mandie put on her coat and tam, grabbed her

books, and rushed to open the front door. Waving goodbye to her parents, she raced outside and up the lane to the main road. Joe was already waiting for her there.

"I was beginning to think you were going to be late," Joe said as he took her books and turned to walk up the road.

"I know," Mandie said with a frown as her short legs tried to keep up with his long ones. "We got into a slow conversation at the table."

Joe glanced down at her. "A slow conversation?"

Mandie looked up at him. "You know, the kind about the long-distant future that will take years to happen."

"What brought that on?" Joe asked. "Are you already planning your adulthood?"

"Oh, Joe Woodard, you know what I mean," Mandie said, with a loud puff of breath. "My father quoted that old saying about going to bed early because I stayed up late reading last night. Then Irene got into the conversation."

Joe slowed as he looked back down the road. "And here comes Irene trying to catch up with us," he remarked.

Mandie turned in time to see her sister rushing up behind them.

As Irene came even with them, she blew out her breath and continued almost running down the road. "Don't wait for me. I'm going to pass you by and get to school early. I want to hurry up and get this day finished," she yelled as she ran on toward the schoolhouse.

"Irene seems to be in an all-fired hurry or something," Joe said as he and Mandie continued on their way.

"I'd say she needs to hurry on a lot of things. She's always late," Mandie replied, watching her sister disappear around the curve.

The two walked on in silence. Mandie kept thinking of the angel and wondering whether to tell Joe about it. After all, she had not made a promise to whoever left the angel that she wouldn't discuss it. And she always told Joe her secrets. He helped her solve the mysteries she was forever running into.

"What are you so quiet about this morning?" Joe asked, suddenly breaking into Mandie's thoughts.

Mandie shrugged. "My mother thinks I stayed up too late last night. I was reading."

"I guess you're tired, then," Joe said.

"I had to go out to the barn and hunt for a button missing from my skirt, too," Mandie said, hurrying to keep up with Joe.

There was no harm in mentioning that as long as she didn't talk about the angel.

"Hunt for a button in the barn at night?" Joe questioned.

"One was missing from my skirt and I couldn't find it in the house, so I went out to the barn and found it where Irene and I had been working—" She stopped as she realized one of the dusters they were making would be for Joe's parents and she wasn't sure she wanted to tell him about it.

"What had you and Irene been working on in the barn?" Joe asked.

"My father is helping us make some Christmas presents. So don't ask any more questions, Joe Woodard, because I am not going to tell you," Mandie replied with a big grin.

"Oh, so Mandie has a secret," Joe teased. "I have a secret, too. The boys are making things we are not going to tell the girls about."

Mandie looked up at him. "I know what you

boys are making. Christmas tree ornaments for Miss Abigail's tree, that's what."

Joe cleared his throat. "That's not all."

They turned in to the lane from the road to the schoolhouse. "Come on. We may be late," Joe said, hastily going up the front steps.

The two removed their coats and hats, hung them on the pegs by the door, and quickly went to their seats. Everyone else was already there.

Suddenly the bell in the little tower on the schoolhouse rang out, beginning the school day. Mandie smoothed down her skirt. It was a close call, but they had made it. She glanced across the room at Joe and grinned. He returned the grin, shaking his head and blowing out his breath.

Mandie tried to keep her mind on her lessons. Then she had a thought. What if whoever had left the angel was in her class? It wasn't likely that one of her young friends would be out late at night. But you never knew. She had found that anything was possible in solving a mystery.

The bell for recess broke into her thoughts. It seemed they had just begun school and here it was, time to eat.

"Come on, Mandie," Faith told her as she stood up from her desk.

"Yes, let's go eat," Esther added as she joined Faith.

Joe was waiting for them outside.

"It's colder than I thought it was," Faith said as she huddled in her coat.

"Sure is," Esther agreed. "Let's hurry and eat and go back inside to warm up." She shivered as she spoke, quickly cramming in a mouthful of biscuit.

"I believe it has dropped a few degrees since we came to school this morning," Joe said as he ate his lunch. "Don't you think so, Mandie?"

"I suppose," she said. "I hadn't noticed."

"I can't wait to get into Miss Abigail's attic," Esther announced. "How about y'all?"

Mandie remembered what her father had said about their own tree. "Guess what?" she told the group.

Everyone was rising to go back inside.

"I don't know what, but let's go back inside to talk," Joe told her.

Everyone had gone back inside to finish out their recess. Mandie looked around at the groups perched here and there on benches at the back and began again. "Guess what, everybody? You are all invited to my house to help decorate our Christmas tree on the Monday night after Miss Abigail's party."

The students began to chatter excitedly. A party was an important part of life at Charley Gap, especially when the younger people were invited.

"Does that include me?" Mr. Tallant asked from his desk at the front of the room. He grinned at Mandie.

"Of course, Mr. Tallant," Mandie said. "It includes everybody who wants to come." Then she added, "I suppose you are going to Miss Abigail's party, too, aren't you?"

"Wouldn't miss it for anything," Mr. Tallant said.

The conversation turned to a discussion of Miss Abigail's attic.

"I'm really anxious to get into Miss Abigail's attic. There's no telling what she has up there," Esther said, rubbing her hands together.

"Maybe even family skeletons," Joe teased.

Everyone gaped at Joe.

Joe looked flustered at the sudden attention. "I was joking, of course. I don't imagine Miss Abigail has any skeletons in her family."

"I hope not," Esther said, shuddering.

"Mandie," Faith spoke up, "Are we supposed to bring anything to your party? Ornaments or anything?"

"No, I don't think so. We have lots of ornaments we've saved for years," Mandie told her. And then she had another thought. "But if your grandmother is back in time, we'd like for you to bring her."

"Oh, yes," echoed the group.

Faith gave Mandie a wistful look. "I'd be glad to if she is, Mandie."

The bell cut the conversation off as recess ended, and everyone returned to their desks.

Mandie wondered what the group would have said about the angel. They would probably ask a thousand questions, she decided. *And the person who put it on our porch might be in this room, or they might be connected with the person who did,* she thought. She was just itching to talk about it; the words were almost floating out of her mouth!

Finally the dismissal bell rang. Faith walked

with them to the crossroad where she turned, and Mandie and Joe hurried on down the road to Mandie's house.

"You've been awfully quiet today," Joe remarked, glancing down at her.

"That's because I don't have anything to say that I can say," Mandie mumbled.

"That doesn't make sense," Joe replied. "You don't have anything to say that you can say? Don't tell me Mandie Shaw is actually speechless."

Mandie stopped in the middle of the road and stomped her foot. "Joe Woodard, you'd be surprised at what I could say, but I can't tell you what it is."

"Mandie, you are not making sense," Joe said. "Do you have a mystery that you are not going to share with me? Is that it?"

Mandie blew out her breath. "Yes. I can't tell you what it is. I'm not supposed to."

"Oh, Mandie, how are you going to solve this mystery all by yourself?" Joe asked teasingly.

"I'll solve it, all right, and then I'll tell you about it," Mandie said, going on down the road.

Joe quickly caught up with her. "Don't forget. That's a promise."

Mandie sighed loudly. "Joe, I've got to hurry home and work on the presents my father is helping me and Irene make," she said.

"All right, all right, I've got to work on mine, too," Joe reminded her.

When they came to the lane leading down off the road to Mandie's house, Mandie took her books from Joe. "Joe, I wish I could tell you about this new secret but I was asked not to tell anyone," she said. "But don't you worry; I will tell you all about it when I get it solved."

Joe was plainly puzzled by Mandie's attitude. He stood there frowning as she walked toward her house. Mandie looked back and waved.

When she reached the house she discovered that Irene had actually arrived home ahead of her. Her sister was in the kitchen, still with her coat and hat on, standing by the cookstove while Mrs. Shaw poured cups of hot coffee.

"Get some coffee before you go out there in that cold barn to work on those dusters," Mrs. Shaw told her.

Mandie hurried into the parlor to leave her books on the table and was turning to go back into the kitchen when she noticed Windy on the hearth playing with something. She bent to inspect it. The cat was batting a bright red ribbon around.

"Windy, where did you get that?" Mandie asked. She remembered the mysterious package on the back porch had been wrapped with a red ribbon.

"Come on, Amanda," Irene called from the kitchen. "We need to get busy and get those old dusters finished once and for all."

Mandie hurried back into the kitchen and asked her mother as she handed her a cup of coffee, "Mama, where did Windy get that red ribbon she is playing with?"

"I have no idea," Mrs. Shaw said as she returned the percolator to the stove. "I let her out this morning and she found it on the porch when I opened the door. Do you know how it got there?"

"Me? Oh, Mama, what would I be doing with a red ribbon on the back porch?" Mandie managed to say, avoiding her mother's gaze.

"I suppose the wind must have blown it there," Mrs. Shaw decided. "Now, you girls, don't stay too long out in that barn. It's too cold and I don't want you two getting sick right here at Christmastime, you hear?"

"Yes, ma'am," Mandie replied. "Is Daddy out there?"

"Yes, he has already brought the turkey feathers from the attic and taken them out to the barn. I gave him some of my bright red knitting yarn to put them together," Mrs. Shaw told her.

"Oh, that's going to be beautiful with the red handles," Mandie exclaimed, gulping down the coffee.

"Come on, Mandie," Irene demanded, going to open the back door. "I'm gone."

Mandie set down the coffee cup and hurried after her sister.

"I'm coming," she called to Irene. As soon as they finished working on the dusters, she would rush back into the house and upstairs to check on the package under her bed.

Who was it from?

5

A Big Problem

"OH, DADDY, THEY are going to be beautiful!" Mandie exclaimed as she surveyed their work. Her father had showed her and Irene how to lay out the feathers and then pull the knitting yarn in and out and around to bind them together in the ridges he had carved into the handles.

"Yes, they do look pretty," Irene agreed.

"And we'll have them finished before suppertime," Mr. Shaw told them. "I'm sure the Woodards and Miss Abigail are going to appreciate these."

"I wonder what they will give us," Irene said, playing with the end of the ball of yarn.

"Irene! You aren't supposed to say that," Mandie rebuked her. "You aren't supposed to give a present in order to receive one back."

"That's not what I said. They always give us something, so I'm just wondering what it will be this year," Irene replied.

"You didn't say it exactly, but that's what you meant," Mandie said.

"Now, girls, let's get these things finished so we can get in the house and warm up," Mr. Shaw told them, reaching for the yarn.

"Yes, let's do," Mandie agreed as she remembered the package under her bed. The sooner they got done, the sooner she could check on it.

The girls threaded pieces of red ribbon through the handles and tied them into bows. Then they stepped back and admired their work.

"Now let's take these dusters in the house and show them to your mother," Mr. Shaw told the girls as he cleaned up the scraps of thread and ribbon.

Mandie and Irene each carried a duster to the house. Mrs. Shaw looked them over and said, "I know these will be appreciated. Now you girls take them upstairs and put them in a safe place until it's time to give out presents and then come back down here to eat your supper." She was

busy ladling up the food from the stove and plac-
ing it on the table.

Up in their room, Mandie looked around for a
place to put the duster she was carrying.

"Let's put them under our beds," Irene suggested, stooping to look under her bed.

"Under the bed?" Mandie repeated anxiously.
"Maybe we ought to hang them up in the closet.
They'd be safer there." She started for the closet
door in the corner.

"But they'll be safe under the bed," Irene insisted as she started to push the duster out of
sight.

"Irene, they'll get dirty under there. I'm going
to hang mine in the closet," Mandie said as she
opened the closet door. She carefully looped the
string in the handle over a nail on the wall.

"Oh, well, I suppose you're right," Irene finally
agreed as she brought hers to the closet and hung
it inside. "At least that cat of yours can't get at it
in there if we keep the door closed."

Mandie watched as Irene closed the closet
door. "Why, Windy wouldn't bother those dusters," she argued.

"You know very well a cat would love to play with those feathers," Irene said. "Now I'm going downstairs to eat."

As soon as Irene left the room, Mandie quickly stooped to look under her bed. The angel package was still there and it didn't seem to have been touched. She gave it a little shove and moved it farther underneath. Then Mandie hurried down to the kitchen, where everyone was waiting for her to sit down and eat.

As they began passing the food around the table, Mrs. Shaw said, "I think we'll skip working on those handkerchiefs tonight and go to bed early. We can continue tomorrow night."

"Good. I'm tired," Irene said. She accepted a bowl of beans from her mother, ladled out some onto her plate, and passed the bowl on to Mandie.

"Mama, we have an awful lot to do on Christmas presents," Mandie reminded her as she put a spoonful of beans on her plate and passed the bowl on to her father.

"And you'll get it done," Mrs. Shaw told her.

After the meal was finished, Mandie gave scraps to Windy in her bowl by the cookstove.

Then she and Irene helped their mother clear off the table and wash the dishes.

As Mandie dried the last plate, Windy went to the back door and meowed. "I'll let you out for a minute or two but don't you run off somewhere," she told the cat as she opened the back door. Windy quickly slipped through and Mandie closed it behind her.

"We'll go in the parlor now while your father reads the Scripture," Mrs. Shaw told the girls as she led the way into the other room.

Mandie had the angel package on her mind and didn't listen to a word her father read. Finally her mother told them to go to bed.

Mandie lay awake a long time thinking about the package and wondering who could have left it on the porch. Through her thoughts, she dimly heard meows coming from outside. *I forgot to let Windy back into the house!* Mandie realized. Careful not to wake her sister, she slipped out of bed and went down to the kitchen. The night was clear and the moon was shining as she quietly opened the back door to let Windy inside.

"Come on," she whispered to the cat as the animal came running into the kitchen. She was about to close the door and lock it when she thought she saw something outside. She held the door open a crack to peer out. Was that another package on the porch? She suddenly felt afraid as she realized there *was* something there. Taking a deep breath, she stooped to reach out through the open door.

"What is this?" she whispered, picking up a small package from the floor of the porch and bringing it inside. She quickly closed the door and sat down on the floor with the bundle.

"Not again," she said under her breath. She quietly opened the brown wrapping paper around the object and pulled out what looked like a jar of jelly. "Now what is this for?" she muttered, moving over to the moonlight coming in through the window. It really was a jar of jelly— and there was also a note wrapped around it. Squinting in the dim light, she made out the words on the paper: *Mandie, This is for you.*

Gathering everything up, Mandie quietly climbed the ladder to her room and slipped the jar under her bed. She got under the covers but was so excited she couldn't sleep.

What was she going to do with the jar of jelly? She figured the sender wanted this kept secret, same as the angel ornament. She wouldn't tell anyone.

Mandie couldn't guess who was leaving these packages on the back porch. There was no way she could have stayed up and watched. Besides, she hadn't known there was going to be a second package left there.

If only she could tell Joe what was going on.

The next morning, when she met Joe at the road to go to school, she had almost decided to tell him everything, regardless of the sender's request that she keep everything secret. She kept reminding herself that she hadn't promised anyone *not* to talk about the mysterious packages.

"Good morning," Mandie greeted Joe as she came up to the road.

"And what are you so happy about this morning?" Joe asked as he took her books.

"Happy?" Mandie asked, hurrying along by his side.

"Happy or excited? You know you can't keep secrets from me," Joe teased her.

"Excited," Mandie immediately replied. "You see, I—" She stopped, deciding not to tell him her secret. Maybe Joe was involved somehow.

"You what, Mandie?" Joe asked.

"I can't tell you yet," Mandie replied, tightening her lips.

"Mandie, why do you have to act so mysterious?" Joe asked, blowing out his breath and causing fog in the cold air. "You might as well go ahead and tell me what it is, because I'll find out anyhow."

"You can't unless I tell you," Mandie said.

Faith met them at the crossroad. She seemed to be excited about something, too.

"I was hoping I would see you before we got to school," Faith told them. "Guess what? Miss Abigail has lost the key to her attic."

"Lost the key to the attic? How are we going to get the Christmas ornaments out of there?" Mandie asked in a disappointed voice as the three of them came to a standstill.

"Nothing to it. Some of the boys and I can just climb up on the porch roof and go in through the window," Joe quickly put in.

"I imagine the windows are locked," Faith said as they continued on their way to the schoolhouse.

"The key has got to be found before the party," Mandie said.

"She's looked everywhere for it," Faith said.

Mandie thought about the angel ornament. If Miss Abigail were unable to have the tree-decorating party, what would she do about the angel?

"Maybe we could help look for the key," Mandie suggested as they turned down the lane to the schoolhouse.

"I asked her that, but she said we wouldn't know any more than she does," Faith explained.

"Maybe we could pick the lock and get it open, or take down the door or something," Joe suggested. "There's bound to be a way to get into the attic."

"Yes, there has got to be a way to get the ornaments out. How can we have the party if we can't get the ornaments out of the attic?" Mandie asked, frustrated.

Faith shrugged as they continued to the porch of the schoolhouse. "Maybe she will find the key before then," she said.

"She has just got to," Mandie said.

They went inside, removed their wraps, hung them on their pegs, and started toward their desks. About half the pupils had arrived.

Esther was already there. "Guess what? Miss Abigail can't have the party because she can't find the key to the attic. Isn't that absolutely awful?"

Mandie looked at her in surprise. "How did you know about it? Faith just now told us."

"Yes, how did you know?" Faith asked. "Miss Abigail only told me this morning."

"Miss Abigail told my mother yesterday at their needlework session," Esther explained. "I think it's ridiculous that anyone would keep their attic locked and then lose the key. Why bother to lock an old attic anyway?"

The other pupils arrived and everyone gathered in the middle of the schoolroom.

Mandie's sister, Irene, came up to them. "Guess we won't be having a party at Miss Abigail's after all," she said.

"We've got to have that party," Mandie said firmly.

"You are having a decorating party at your

house, Mandie," Esther reminded her. "We don't *have* to have a party at Miss Abigail's."

"That's right," Joe agreed.

"No, no, we have to have a party at Miss Abigail's," Mandie repeated, raising her voice.

"No, we don't," Joe said. "Miss Abigail can come to your party instead."

"No, you don't understand. We have to have that party at Miss Abigail's," Mandie insisted.

All the other young people had stopped talking and turned to look at Mandie. What could she tell them? The angel ornament was a secret and it was also important.

The bell suddenly rang, calling the class to order. Everyone rushed to their desks. Mandie went to sit down and tried to figure out how the key to Miss Abigail's attic could be found.

Mr. Tallant called the roll and then spoke to the class. "I heard about the lost key to Miss Abigail's attic. I would like to suggest that we all get together and put up the tree for the church instead. Every year Preacher Mahon does this alone, so I know he would appreciate any help this group could give him. What do y'all say to that?"

There were eager replies across the room as the pupils agreed that this was an exciting possibility.

Mandie, however, was not satisfied. What on earth would she do about the Christmas ornament? It was supposed to go on *Miss Abigail's* tree.

Suddenly she had another idea. Miss Abigail always attended the church service for Christmas, like everyone else in Charley Gap did. She could put the angel on the church tree. Miss Abigail would certainly see it on there.

"But the note said put it on *her* tree," she muttered to herself. Maybe she could just leave the ornament on Miss Abigail's doorstep like someone had left it on hers. She'd have to go off by herself to a quiet place and think about the problem. She'd figure it all out somehow.

6

A Solution

THAT WEEKEND MR. TALLANT and all his pupils helped Preacher Mahon put up the huge cedar tree in the church. Decorations were donated by every family in Charley Gap. Almost everyone attended this church—the next nearest one was way over the mountain, and in bad weather that was too far to travel.

All the helpers had brought food from home. They gathered around the table in a corner of the sanctuary to have their party.

"It really is a beautiful tree," Mandie said as she picked up a cup of hot cocoa.

"Yes, it is. But no one brought anything for the top," Faith said, pointing to the bare treetop. "We really need something up there, don't you think?"

Mandie frowned as she thought about the angel. "Yes, it does need something. Maybe someone has something we could add." She glanced around among her friends standing by the table.

"I'll ask my mother for something to put up there," Esther spoke up. "We have more ornaments than we ever use."

"Like what?" Mandie asked.

"Lots of little things we've collected, from as far back as I can remember," Esther said.

"Do you think you might have an extra angel or a star? That's what would really look nice up there," Joe suggested.

There's no way he could know about the angel I found on our doorstep—unless maybe he is the one who put it there, Mandie thought.

"The boys are making ornaments for Miss Abigail's tree, but if she isn't going to have one, we could use some of them on this one," Joe told the girls. "And I believe one of the boys is carving an angel to put on her tree."

"That would be nice," Faith said.

"But we haven't completely given up on Miss Abigail's having a tree yet, have we? I mean, maybe the key will be found," Mandie reminded her friends.

"Well, if someone doesn't hurry up and find

that key, it's going to be too late to have the party," Esther said, picking up a cookie from a plate on the table.

"I'm not going to give up on finding it until the very last minute," Mandie said, frowning as she wondered what she would do with the angel if Miss Abigail didn't have the party. It would look nice on the church tree. But suppose then Miss Abigail found the key and went ahead and had her party! Then what would she do?

After she went home that night, Mandie did some more thinking. She was aggravated by the fact that she didn't know who had left the angel.

And she decided she was not going to play any more games with whoever had done it.

After everyone had gone to bed and she was sure her sister was asleep, Mandie crept downstairs to get a piece of paper and a pencil. In the dim moonlight shining through the kitchen window, she quickly wrote a note.

Whoever has been leaving things on our back porch, this is to ask you not to leave anything else, or I will tell. Miss Abigail has lost the key to

*the attic and now I don't know what to do with
the angel.*

Mandie Shaw

She silently opened the back door and propped the note up beside some pieces of pine kindling on the porch, making sure to place it where it wouldn't blow away but where it could be seen. Stepping back into the kitchen, she softly closed the door and stood there a minute, thinking.

"What if no one comes tonight and gets the note?" she wondered. "Daddy will find it in the morning if it's still there." She sighed and went back upstairs to bed. After worrying about it for a while, she finally went to sleep.

The old rooster crowing in the backyard woke her the next morning. She immediately remembered her note and hurried to shed her nightgown and put on her clothes, hoping to get downstairs before her father went outside. She smelled coffee perking and knew he was already in the kitchen.

"Good morning, my little blue-eyes," Mr.

Shaw said as Mandie came into the room. He was standing by the iron cookstove waiting for the coffee.

"Good morning, Daddy," Mandie replied, looking anxiously at the back door. "Have you been outside this morning? I mean, is it cold outside?" She quickly walked over to the back door.

"No, I haven't even unlatched the door yet. You're up early," Mr. Shaw told her, turning to pour a cup of hot coffee.

Mandie reached to flip the latch on the door, opened it a few inches, and glanced outside. The note was gone, thank goodness! She took a deep breath and closed the door. "It is cold out there."

"After all, it is December," Mr. Shaw told her. Turning back to the stove, he picked up another cup from the shelf above it and filled it with coffee. "Here, have some coffee and you'll warm up."

Mandie smiled at her tall, red-haired, blue-eyed father as she took the cup. "Thank you, Daddy," she said, going to sit down at the table.

"Don't forget now, we'll go out and find our tree this coming Saturday and we'll put it up on Monday," he reminded her as he sat down, too.

"Too bad Miss Abigail is not having her party," Mandie said, feeling disappointed. "It was supposed to have been Saturday, remember?"

"How could I forget, with everyone talking about it?" Mr. Shaw replied with a big smile. "Who knows? Maybe she'll find that key before then."

"We've all offered to help her search for it but she won't let us," Mandie told him, warming her hands on the cup.

"I believe the whole community has offered to help look. She could have a tree without getting into her attic, after all," Mr. Shaw said. "Everyone has offered to donate an ornament, too, and that would be more than enough to cover the tree. But she is one stubborn lady." He shook his head as he smiled.

Windy woke up and hopped out of the woodbox. She licked her face and then came to sit down at Mandie's feet. Mandie bent to rub her head.

"I think Windy chased a mouse last night," Mr. Shaw said. "I heard some sound here in the kitchen after we went to bed but didn't get up to investigate." He looked straight at Mandie.

Mandie dropped her eyes. Had her father heard her in the kitchen? Did he suspect that she had made the noise? She had tried to be quiet and thought she had been practically noiseless. "I didn't hear a thing," she said without looking at him.

"We're almost finished with Faith's grandmother's house," Mr. Shaw told her. "Miss Abigail has been keeping Faith away so it will be a big surprise when her grandmother returns home. Has Faith asked you anything about the work we're doing?"

"No, Daddy, she never mentions the house. She just wishes her grandmother could get some help in New York, and she wishes that it would happen in a hurry so she can come back home," Mandie told him.

"I understand. Dr. Woodard thinks those New York doctors will be able to help her some, but he's not sure how much," Mr. Shaw said, sipping his hot coffee. "Even a little bit will be a great blessing for the poor woman."

"That would be wonderful," Mandie agreed. Changing the subject to what was really on her mind, she asked, "Do you think someone just might find Miss Abigail's key?"

Mr. Shaw smiled at her. "Maybe. It has to be in her house somewhere. If she'd just let someone help look, it might be found." He stood up and finished the last sip of his coffee. "Now why don't we start breakfast?"

"Good idea," Mandie agreed, swallowing her coffee and rising to join him. "I suddenly realize I'm starving."

Later, after they had all had breakfast, Mandie met Joe up at the road and walked to school with him. Irene hurried on ahead.

"Cheer up, things couldn't get worse," Joe told her with a big grin as Mandie silently walked down the road with him.

Mandie looked up at him. "Things couldn't get worse? Now what has happened?"

"Nothing new. It's the same old story, the missing key," Joe teased her.

"I don't care about the key if only Miss Abigail would just have a tree-decorating party anyhow. We could bring all the ornaments," Mandie told him.

"I know, I know, same old story," Joe said. "Let's forget Miss Abigail if she wants to be stubborn like that. Let's talk about your party. It's still planned for next Monday night, isn't it?"

"Yes, my father reminded me this morning,"

Mandie said. "This has become the most mixed-up mess, and everybody is talking about it. I'll really be glad when Christmas is over."

Joe slowed his steps. "Mandie! You don't mean that!" he protested. "You always enjoy Christmastime."

"I know, but we've never had Miss Abigail involved before. She has always stayed in her big fine house and never joined our parties. Now all of a sudden she wants to have a party and then loses the key and then cancels the party. That's not fair," Mandie said, stomping her feet as she walked.

"Have you invited Miss Abigail to your party?" Joe asked as they continued down the road.

"My mother and father said to ask all our school friends. They didn't say anything about Miss Abigail," Mandie said, frowning as she thought about it. "Why should we ask Miss Abigail to our party?"

"Amanda Elizabeth Shaw, you are thick-headed sometimes," Joe declared. "Miss Abigail asked us to her party—shouldn't you ask her to yours?"

"I'll have to ask my parents," Mandie told him.

"They may be inviting other adults," Joe suggested, as they stepped up onto the front porch of the schoolhouse. "Especially since it's at night and the parents will have to bring their children anyway."

"Have they invited your parents?" Mandie asked as Joe opened the door.

"I don't know. I'll find out," Joe promised.

The other pupils gathered around Mandie as she entered. Her family's party was the next interesting event coming up and they all wanted to talk about it.

"When are you going to get your tree?" Aaron asked.

"Who is going with you to get the tree?" Esther wanted to know.

"Maybe we could all join you in the search?" Tommy Lester asked, looking at Irene, who was standing across the room.

"It has always just been my father and Irene and me," Mandie told the group. "My father says it's a family tradition."

"Your mother is not going with you?" Aaron asked.

Mandie laughed. "She doesn't want to ramble around out there in those cold woods looking for a tree."

At that moment Mr. Tallant tapped on his desk and said, "Aaron, have you forgotten? It's time to ring the bell."

"Yes sir, Mr. Tallant," Aaron replied, and started toward the door.

Aaron usually rang the bell because he was the tallest and strongest of all the pupils. Moments later, as the big iron bell rang out on the front porch of the schoolhouse, the students scrambled for their desks.

Mr. Tallant then called the roll and made an announcement. "As you all know, Friday will be the last day of school before the holidays," he told them. "We need to finish up our chapters in reading and in arithmetic, so we'll do that in class instead of my giving you any homework. Then when we return after Christmas, we'll get started on new chapters."

As Mr. Tallant called on various pupils to read aloud to the class, Mandie's mind wandered to the angel ornament. She couldn't decide what to do with it. Oh, this angel was causing a lot of problems. She wished she could discuss it with her father, the way she usually did when she was confronted with a problem. Maybe whoever it was wouldn't know if she told her father? Mandie sighed. If only Miss Abigail would just have a party!

After school, Mandie and Irene worked with their mother on the handkerchiefs they were making for presents. As they sat around the kitchen table, Irene asked the question Mandie wanted answered. "Are parents coming to our Christmas tree–decorating party next Monday night, or just the pupils in our school?" she asked as she stopped her needlework and looked up at her mother.

"Some of the parents will be here. You young people can't travel around at night alone," Mrs. Shaw said, checking Irene's work. "Now be careful with your stitches there."

"Will Miss Abigail come with Faith?" Mandie asked.

"We asked her," Mrs. Shaw replied.

Then Mandie made up her mind about the angel ornament. She would just put it on the top of their tree and Miss Abigail would see it there. She was going to quit worrying. After all, whoever left it caused this trouble. It wasn't her problem.

But the situation changed later that night. Everyone had gone to bed, but Mandie couldn't sleep. She kept turning over and over under the heavy quilts. Windy, sleeping at her feet, meowed as she was tossed about. Out of the corner of her eye, Mandie thought she could see snowflakes falling outside the window. She silently got up and went to the window to look. There were a few scattered flakes.

"The snow won't stay," Mandie mumbled as she turned to get back into bed. But then she saw something move in the yard. She leaned against the window to see out. She was sure she saw someone run across the yard.

"That's him!" Mandie whispered excitedly as she hurried to get downstairs. That was the person leaving the things on her back porch!

"Hurry, hurry, hurry!" she breathed as she raced for the back door and silently opened it to look out.

Sure enough, there was a package leaning against the pile of kindling on the porch. She excitedly reached for it and backed into the house, closing the door against the cold air.

Not daring to light a lamp for fear of waking someone, Mandie quickly opened the brown wrapping. This was a small package and didn't seem to weigh very much—not another ornament, she hoped. And she remembered her note to this gift-giver, saying she would tell if he left anything else. Well, she would see what this was and then she would tell someone, probably her father.

When she finally got the paper opened, she was excited to find a big old skeleton key. She knew right away that it must be the key to Miss Abigail's attic, and in the faint light from the cookstove she made out the writing on the note attached to the key:

Here is the key to Miss Abigail's attic. Just leave it on her hall table and she'll find it.

"Now she can have the party!" Mandie exclaimed as she quietly rolled up the paper, held tightly to the key, and hurried back to bed.

That night she went to sleep with the key under her pillow.

7

Complications

THE NEXT MORNING at the breakfast table, Mandie asked permission to go home with Faith after school. She had the key in her skirt pocket.

"Amanda, we still have lots of work to do on your Christmas presents," her mother reminded her, looking up from her plate of grits.

"I won't stay very long, and I'll ask Joe to go with me," Mandie replied, almost holding her breath in fear of her mother's denying her permission. "Please, Mama." She squeezed her coffee cup with both hands.

"All right, Amanda," Mrs. Shaw said. "But mind you, you'd better not stay over thirty minutes, you hear?"

Mandie settled back in her seat. "Yes, ma'am. Thank you, Mama."

That was one hurdle over with. Now she would have to talk Joe into walking with her to Faith's house. She knew he was busy with the woodworking classes after school on certain days, and today was probably one of them.

After breakfast was finished, Mandie put on her coat and tam, grabbed her books, and raced up the lane to the main road. Joe was waiting, as usual. She never managed to get there first.

"In a hurry?" Joe asked, as he took her books.

Mandie blew out her breath, making fog in the cold air. "Oh, this is going to be a fast day."

"And what is going to make it a fast day?" Joe asked.

"I have permission to walk home with Faith, but I can only stay thirty minutes. Joe, please walk with me. I told my mother you would," Mandie begged, looking up with her blue eyes.

"Wait a minute," Joe said, slowing down. "You told your mother I would walk with you to Faith's house? You haven't exactly asked me if I would. I don't like being manipulated."

"If that big word means bossing you around, I'm not doing that, Joe," Mandie protested. "I'm only hoping you will walk with me because you

know my mother doesn't want me going any-
where alone."

"But you have to ask me first. You can't go
around telling me what to do," Joe said with a
frown.

"All right! Joe Woodard, will you walk with me
so I can go home with Faith and stay thirty minutes and then go home myself?" Mandie asked in
one big breath, coming to a halt in the middle of
the road.

Joe rubbed his chin. "All right, you asked. All
right, I will walk with you," he said. "You'd better
be glad this afternoon isn't one of our woodworking days."

Mandie hurried to catch up with him and gave
his hand a tug. She knew she could count on Joe.

At school, Mandie had another problem. She
had to ask Faith if she and Joe could walk home
with her. Faith was going to wonder why.

At recess while they were eating lunch together, Mandie asked, "Could Joe and I walk
home with you after school?"

Faith took a small bite of her apple. "Is something special going on?" she asked. "I mean, is
there a reason to walk home with me today?"

Mandie smiled at her. "Do we have to have a reason to walk together? I just thought it would give us a chance to talk about things, like the Christmas party at my house."

Faith smiled back. "Of course, Mandie. We've all been so busy making presents we haven't had much time together lately," she said, her dark eyes warm. "Sure, come on with me, and I'm sure Miss Abigail will make us all a cup of tea."

Mandie debated telling Faith about the key but then decided not to. She had not even told Joe.

Just like Mandie had predicted to Joe, the school day passed quickly. Everyone was in a holiday spirit, and Mr. Tallant was lax with his rules. He pretended not to notice when someone whispered or motioned to someone else across the room.

As soon as Mr. Tallant dismissed them, Mandie, Joe, and Faith raced for their coats and hats and beat the rush out the door.

As the three walked down the long curving road in the shadows of the Nantahala Mountains, Mandie tried to think of something to talk about. She was so excited about the key she could think of nothing else.

"Is Miss Abigail coming to Mandie's party with you?" Joe asked Faith.

"She hasn't decided yet. She's so upset about having to cancel her own party that she can't talk about anything else," Faith said.

Mandie looked at Faith and smiled. How she wished she could just say, "Here's the key! Now Miss Abigail can have her party!" But she would put it on the hall table, as she'd been instructed.

When they arrived at Miss Abigail's house, the lady was sitting by the fireplace in the parlor, reading. She looked up and smiled as the three came into the room. "Why it's nice to see you, Amanda, and Joe, too! Sit down. I'll have Miss Dicey brew a pot of tea," she greeted them, rising and closing her book. "Take off your coats."

"I can only stay thirty minutes, Miss Abigail. I have to work on my Christmas presents," Mandie said, hastily unbuttoning her coat.

"And I'm with her," Joe added with a big grin as he removed his coat.

Miss Abigail went out into the hall. "I'll be right back."

Mandie and Joe hung their coats on the coatrack in the hall and Faith added hers. They went back into the parlor and pulled chairs up near the fireplace. They talked about their schoolwork and the coming holidays.

Soon Miss Abigail returned. Miss Dicey followed, carrying a tray that she placed on a nearby table. While they were being served tea and sweet biscuits, Mandie felt the key in her skirt pocket and wondered how she would be able to place it on the hall table.

Suddenly luck came her way. "Ah-choo!" she sneezed loudly.

"Excuse me. I have to get my handkerchief out of my coat pocket," she said, jumping up to run out into the hall. She fished the key out of her deep skirt pocket and quickly laid it in a crystal tray on the hall table. Snatching her handkerchief from her coat pocket, she rushed back to the parlor, where she sneezed again. Something was really making her sneeze, but she didn't mind. It had served her purpose perfectly.

After a short visit, Mandie and Joe got their coats and left. Mandie kept watching the table to see if anyone noticed the key, but Miss Abigail was busy bidding them goodbye.

The next day word got around. Miss Abigail had found her key and the party was rescheduled for the coming Saturday night. Everyone was excited.

School was out for the holidays on Friday, and all the young people made promises to attend Miss Abigail's party and also the Shaws', which would be the next Monday night.

On Saturday Mandie and Irene went with their father into the wooded area at the back of their farm and found a beautiful cedar tree for Christmas. They left it in the barn until Mr. Shaw could put it up for their party.

And then everyone got ready for Miss Abigail's party. Mandie wore a lovely burgundy velvet dress, one of her few Sunday dresses. Miss Abigail met them at the door, and sent the young people into the library at the back of the house to wait for everyone to arrive. The adults gathered in the parlor. Mandie had carefully concealed the angel in a flour sack under her coat in the hall.

"Oh, I can't wait to get into Miss Abigail's attic and see what's in there," Mandie remarked, walking around the room.

"Probably just a lot of old furniture and boxes and stuff like that," Esther said, perching on the straight chair by the long library table.

"Yes, a lot of junk," Irene added. She and Tommy Lester stood by the mantelpiece.

"And broken-down furniture and old dusty trunks," Joe said.

"The graveyard for things you don't want anymore," Aaron said, joining Joe by the doorway.

"You will probably all be surprised," Faith said, with a little laugh. She looked beautiful in her blue dress with a lace collar. She walked around the room.

"I would never be surprised by anything concerning Miss Abigail," Tommy Lester remarked.

As soon as all the pupils from Mr. Tallant's school had arrived, Faith went to let Miss Abigail know. The lady came back with her and stopped in the doorway to speak to the group.

"Faith will take you all up to the attic," she said. "Please don't bring everything down at one time, but just as you need it. The tree is already standing in the parlor and the grown-ups will move on into the sitting room to get out of your way." She turned to leave. "Have fun," she added, her eyes twinkling.

Faith led the way upstairs and on up another flight of steps from the upper hallway. The door at the top was closed and she pushed it open, stepping back so the young people could enter the attic.

Mandie quickly looked around the huge room. The place was well lighted with lamps here and there. And as Faith had said, they were all surprised. The entire room was empty except for four trunks standing near the doorway: two small ones and two huge steamer trunks.

"Is this all that's up here?" Mandie asked Faith.

"Yes, and the decorations are in the trunks," Faith explained. "She showed me the attic earlier today."

"Four trunks full of Christmas decorations?" Joe questioned.

"Where's all the stuff that supposed to be in an attic?" Tommy Lester asked.

"Miss Abigail told me she uses everything that she wants to keep and gets rid of other things, rather than cluttering up an attic," Faith replied.

Joe raised the lid of one of the larger trunks and the other boys opened the others. The girls began pulling out decorations.

"Everybody get something and we'll take it downstairs to the tree and then keep coming back for more," Faith told them.

As the group made several trips up and down the stairs Mandie kept watching to see if anyone had found anything for the treetop. So far no one had.

Then the sound of music filled the air. Mandie realized there must be a piano somewhere in the house; she had never seen it. The group started singing carols with the music, and on her third trip down the stairs Mandie slipped away from the crowd in the direction of the music. She found Miss Abigail playing the piano in a small sitting room at the back of the house. Without being seen, Mandie quickly rejoined her friends and spread the word as to the source of the music.

"Miss Abigail is an amazing lady," Mandie remarked to Faith as they went back up the stairs together for more decorations. "I didn't know she could play the piano—or even that she had one!"

"She certainly is. That room with the piano

has been locked ever since I've been staying here. I didn't even know about it," Faith replied.

Mandie looked at her friend and grinned. "That lady sure does like keys and things locked up, doesn't she?" she remarked.

"Definitely," Faith agreed, as they came to the top of the stairs.

On her next trip down, Mandie found Miss Abigail standing in the doorway watching the group decorating the tree. Then she realized the music was still playing but Miss Abigail was standing right there. Mandie turned to Joe behind her. "I wonder who is playing the piano now."

Joe grinned. "My mother, of course. Remember she used to be a music teacher?"

"Oh, that's right," Mandie replied. "Let's go down the hallway and go through the other doorway," Mandie said. "That way we won't have to pass Miss Abigail."

"All right," Joe agreed, following Mandie down the hallway to the other door.

Mandie stopped there and handed Joe the garlands that she was carrying. "Would you please take these? I brought something for the top of the tree and I'll get it."

Joe took the decorations and waited as Mandie went to her coat and took out the flour sack containing the angel. She hurried back to join him. "Come on and help me put this on top of the tree."

"What is it?" Joe asked, following Mandie into the room.

"Something special," Mandie said under her breath. "Don't say anything to Miss Abigail but help me get it up on top of the tree."

Joe walked over to the tree and stood by the ladder they had been using to reach the top branches. "Mandie has something for the top," he told Faith. "Want to help get it up?"

"Sure," Faith said.

Mandie carefully took the angel out of the flour sack. She handed the sack to Joe. Faith held the ladder steady as Mandie climbed up to place the ornament on top. She tried to watch Miss Abigail out of the corner of her eye, but she had to watch her step as she raised the angel in the air in an effort to fasten it to the top limb.

"Just what it needed," Joe remarked as the group stopped work and watched.

"Yes," everyone agreed.

Just as Mandie managed to get the angel to stay put, Miss Abigail came rushing across the room. "Where did you get that? Where?" she demanded in a tremulous voice, as she stood by the ladder.

Mandie carefully descended the ladder. She didn't reply.

"Amanda, I asked you where you got that ornament," Miss Abigail insisted.

"Was it not with the other ornaments, Miss Abigail?" Mandie asked uncomfortably, as she stepped down onto the floor. She was really frightened now. Miss Abigail seemed to be awfully upset.

"No, it was not. That angel was missing before I moved here to Charley Gap," Miss Abigail said. "Amanda, I insist. Where did you get it?"

"I don't know, Miss Abigail," Mandie replied and secretly decided she was telling the truth. "You have so many ornaments and everything."

Miss Abigail turned to look at the other young people. "Do any of you know where the angel came from?" she asked.

Everyone had become quiet. They shook their heads.

"Oh, dear," Miss Abigail said to herself and rushed out of the room.

Everyone looked at everyone else. Joe gave Mandie a glance and frowned. Mandie straightened her shoulders and stood back to survey the tree. "It's absolutely beautiful, isn't it?" she said to the group, trying to cheer herself. She hated to upset Miss Abigail, but she couldn't reveal her secret, could she?

"Yes," went around the room. Soon they all joined in the singing again as the piano continued in the other room.

"Just where did you get that angel?" Joe asked Mandie later while they were drinking eggnog.

"I really don't know," Mandie whispered back.

"You must know. You brought it with you," he argued.

"But I don't know where it came from," Mandie argued back. "I'll explain later." She started mingling with the crowd. No one else asked any questions, and Mandie figured they all thought she had found the angel in one of the trunks.

Miss Abigail finally returned to join them. She chatted with her guests and seemed calm once more.

Mandie couldn't figure it out. If that angel had belonged to Miss Abigail years ago and had disappeared, then someone must have stolen it and then decided to return it. But why bring it back after all those years? And who was it who had left it on her back porch?

8

Merry Christmas!

THE FOLLOWING MONDAY night the Shaws had *their* tree-decorating party. Miss Abigail did not attend. Mandie wondered if the lady was angry with her. The Woodards picked up Faith and brought her with them.

"Why didn't Miss Abigail come to our party? Is she mad at me about the angel?" Mandie asked.

"She was not feeling well," Faith explained. "She has not even mentioned the angel to me, but I believe it would cheer her up if you would explain where you got it."

"Please don't tell anyone about this, but I just don't know where the angel came from. I found it on our back porch one night," Mandie whispered, glancing around the room to be sure no one else heard her.

"You mean someone left it on your back porch?" Faith asked, her eyes wide.

"Yes, but I don't know who it was," Mandie replied. "Anyhow, this is all a secret. I am trying to solve the mystery and will let you know if I do."

"Oh, yes, please do," Faith quickly told her. "And I won't tell a single soul what you have told me."

Mandie did not mention the note that had been with it. Now that Miss Abigail had the angel, she didn't know what she could do to investigate, but she would keep thinking about it. Maybe one day she would find out more about the angel and the person who had left it.

Christmas Day finally came, and with it a beautiful snowstorm. Such a thing didn't daunt the people of Charley Gap. They were used to heavy snow and ice in that part of the mountains. They just kept right on going.

When Mandie woke that morning she heard her father in the kitchen stoking the stove. The aroma of perking coffee rose to greet her. Remembering that it was Christmas Day, she jumped out of bed and hurried to get dressed. Then she reached over to shake her sister.

"Irene, it's Christmas! Get up. Daddy is already down in the kitchen," Mandie told her.

For once, Irene didn't growl back at her upon being awakened. She sat up in bed, rubbed her eyes, and stepped out onto the bare floor. "I'll be down in a couple of minutes," she told Mandie as she reached for her clothes.

"I'm going on downstairs," Mandie said.

Mrs. Shaw was in the kitchen cooking breakfast.

"Merry Christmas, Amanda."

"Merry Christmas, Mama," Mandie said. Her father turned to speak to her.

"I don't believe the snow will keep us in today, so as soon as we eat I'll find out if Preacher Mahon is still planning to have a service this morning. If so, we'll go and then make our rounds to give out presents afterward. If there is no church service, why then we'll just start our visits."

"I'm glad we can still get out," Mandie said with a big smile. She went to the dish cupboard and took down the plates, cups, and saucers to set the table. "Mmmm! That bacon sure smells good. I hope you're cooking a lot, Mama, because I believe I could eat a panful myself."

"I sure am," her mother said. "It's Christmas Day, and there's no telling who might come by for a bite to eat."

"Especially that Woodard boy," Mr. Shaw said, bending to look out into the backyard through the window.

Mandie hurried over to look for herself and sure enough, there was Joe, alighting from his horse with his arms full of gifts. "My goodness, Joe is out awfully early this morning," she remarked and went to open the back door.

"Merry Christmas!" Joe greeted her as he stomped the snow off his shoes and came into the kitchen. "Merry Christmas, Mrs. Shaw, Mr. Shaw." He piled the presents on the sideboard and unbuttoned his coat.

"Merry Christmas, Joe," Mr. Shaw returned. "We almost have breakfast done. Why don't you run and put the horse in the barn so you can stay awhile and eat a bite?"

Joe grinned up at the tall, red-haired man. "Oh, thank you, Mr. Shaw. I'll do just that. Be back in a minute." He rushed back out the door.

"Since he brought all those gifts himself, I

don't imagine his parents will be coming over," Mrs. Shaw said, glancing at the pile.

"My father had to go over the mountain early this morning to see about old Mr. Corn," Joe explained when he returned to the kitchen. "He fell and got a little hurt yesterday, and my father wanted to be sure he was all right, since he's alone over there—and it is Christmas Day, too. So Mother sent some food and a gift."

"Hang your things on the pegs back there so they'll be dry when you leave," Mrs. Shaw told him, pointing to the hooks near the stove.

"Yes, ma'am," Joe agreed and hung everything up.

Irene came into the room and everyone sat down at the table.

"How are the roads?" Mr. Shaw asked, passing the huge platter of bacon around the table.

"Not really bad on horseback, and I'd say you won't have any trouble with your wagon either, if it doesn't turn worse," Joe replied, lifting several slices of the bacon onto his plate.

"Good," Mr. Shaw said. "Had any word about church yet?"

"Preacher Mahon told my father early this morning that they would just keep the doors open all day and anyone who wants to can come in. If a big enough crowd shows up at regular preaching time, why then he'll give a sermon," Joe explained.

"Then as soon as we are finished here, we'll go on with our plans to make calls and go to church," Mr. Shaw said.

Mandie was itching with impatience to get into the pile of presents Joe had brought. She had knitted him a scarf. It was wrapped up under the Christmas tree in the parlor. So was the feather duster she and Irene had made for his parents.

Joe caught Mandie looking across the room at the presents. He smiled. "That largest one is for Windy."

"Windy?" Mandie repeated.

"Yes, and the tiniest one is for you," he said, still smiling. He devoured the grits on his plate and ate the bacon with a hot biscuit.

Mandie thought about that for a minute. What could be in a tiny package?

They began with Joe's gifts. Mandie opened the one addressed to Windy and held up a large handmade basket with a soft lining in it. "A new bed for Windy," Joe explained.

"How nice! Thank you, from Windy," Mandie said, setting it down beside the woodbox. "I'll put it here, and when she gets used to it I'll move it behind the stove where it's warmer."

Mr. and Mrs. Shaw unwrapped presents he had brought for them and found sweaters knitted by Mrs. Woodard for each of them. Irene received a new leather strap for carrying her school books. Joe had made it.

"Now you are last," Joe teased Mandie and handed her a small present.

Mandie looked at it and then pulled off the wrapping paper. Inside was a tiny carved angel, painted white and gold. "Oh, Joe, thank you so much," she said excitedly. "I'll hang it by my mirror upstairs, where I can always see it." She held it up by the ribbon attached to it.

At that moment wagon wheels were heard in the yard and everyone turned to look out the window.

"Why that's Miss Abigail—and she's with a strange man!" Mandie said, going near the window to look outside.

Mr. Shaw opened the back door as Miss Abigail and the man stepped up onto the porch. "Come in the house. Merry Christmas to y'all."

"And Merry Christmas to y'all," Miss Abigail replied, leading the way into the kitchen. "Oh, it's so nice and warm in here." She went over to the stove to warm her hands.

The stranger shook hands with Mr. Shaw. Everyone stared at him. He was tall, good-looking, and well dressed. And he was looking directly at Mandie with a smile so big she was afraid his thin mustache was going to pop right off his face! His arms were full of presents. She felt flustered and turned to look at Miss Abigail by the stove.

Miss Abigail had spotted the angel Mandie was still holding by the ribbon. She came over to inspect it. "This is beautiful, Amanda," she said. "Now you have an angel of your very own."

Miss Abigail still had not introduced the man. Mr. Shaw kept looking from one to the other and finally said, "Why don't we all sit down over here at the table and have a cup of coffee. I just made a new pot."

"Yes, remove your wraps and stay awhile,"

Mrs. Shaw added. "Pegs there by the door." She pointed.

Miss Abigail took off her coat, hat, and gloves, and the man removed his and helped her hang them on the pegs. They went over to sit at the table.

Mandie snuck a peek at Joe and he grinned at her. He was wondering who the man was, too.

Then, with her usual brazen attitude, Irene asked, "Miss Abigail, is this man your new feller?"

Miss Abigail and the man howled at that remark. Miss Abigail had to wipe tears from her eyes, she laughed so much. Finally she recovered her voice. "No, Irene, this is not my fellow," she said. "This is my long lost brother—"

"Brother?" Mandie interrupted in her excitement. Miss Abigail actually had some relatives after all!

"Yes, Amanda," Miss Abigail said. "This is my brother, Charlie. We haven't seen each other for years."

"Then you're not from around here, sir," Mr. Shaw said, trying to make conversation.

"No, I've never been here before. It took me several years to even find this place on the map after I learned that Abigail had moved here," Charlie said.

"Plan to stay awhile?" Mr. Shaw asked.

Charlie looked at Mandie, then at Miss Abigail, and replied, "I've been here awhile already, although no one was aware of it."

Mandie gasped as she suddenly figured out who he was. He was the person who had been leaving things on her back porch! But why?

"You left the angel?" Mandie asked.

Everyone looked at her, not understanding what she was talking about, except for Miss Abigail, who smiled at Mandie and then at Charlie.

"Yes, missy, I did," Charlie said.

"The angel that Amanda put on my tree was the one that Charlie took with him when he left home years ago," Miss Abigail explained. "We had had a spat and then lost track of each other."

"How wonderful you are reunited!" Mrs. Shaw said, smiling at the two.

"A spat?" Irene asked.

"Yes, an adult kind of disagreement," Miss Abigail told her.

"And when I found out where she was, I managed to stay in her attic without her knowing it until she finally missed the key, and I had to leave that for Mandie to return to her so she could have that Christmas party," Charlie explained.

"Yes, and you caused me to get upset with Amanda about the angel because she said she didn't know where it came from—and she really didn't!" Miss Abigail said.

"Sorry about that, Sis, but I was so overjoyed at finding you, I couldn't think straight as to how I would actually speak to you. I knew you would recognize the angel," Charlie explained.

"Oh, you should have seen her when she saw it on the tree." Joe spoke up. "I was afraid she was going to collapse."

"Anyhow, now we've settled all our disagreements," Miss Abigail said. "And we've brought some presents for everybody."

"Why didn't Faith come with you?" Mandie asked.

"Oh, I'm sorry. I forgot the big news!" Miss Abigail put her hand on Mandie's arm. "Her grandmother arrived from New York—and her face is in *much* better shape. She is staying at my house with Faith tonight. Mr. Shaw, we wanted you men to take her to her house and surprise her with all you've done."

"Now Christmas is complete!" Mandie burst out.

"Yes, I'll get some of the other men who worked on the house to come with me whenever you say, Miss Abigail," Mr. Shaw said.

Charlie stood up and went over to pick up one of the gifts he had deposited on the sideboard. Going directly to Mandie, he said, "This is a special present for you, young lady. I will always be grateful for your cooperation in my plot."

Mandie took the present. It was heavy. She turned it over and over.

"Well, open it," Irene called to her.

Mandie quickly removed the wrapping and found a white box. Removing the lid on that, she stared at a beautiful silver-framed hand mirror and matching comb and brush. She started crying in spite of herself. Joe rushed to put an arm around her shoulders.

"Hey, you aren't supposed to cry when people give you presents," he teased. "You're supposed to say thank you."

Mandie laughed through her tears and ran to Charlie. She squeezed his hand. "It's the most beautiful thing I have ever owned. Thank you!"

"I knew you'd like it," Charlie whispered as he squeezed her hand back.

Then, remembering the angel from Joe, she picked it up from the table where she had laid it. "And this is also the most beautiful present I have ever received."

Joe rushed to her side again and put his arm around her shoulders for a big squeeze.

"Now that that's all done, I'd like to say something myself," Miss Abigail said. "This is the most wonderful Christmas I have ever had, all because of you, Amanda."

"Merry Christmas from Mandie!" Charlie declared.

Mandie would long remember that day as one of the most special in her life. And she supposed she had helped in a tiny way to make such a wonderful holiday for Miss Abigail and Charlie.

Suddenly giggly with excitement, Mandie turned to Joe, planted a quick kiss on his cheek and said, "Merry Christmas, Joe, from Mandie."

Personalized Christmas Ornament

As Mandie knows, an ornament can be a wonderful gift. Personalizing it makes it even more special. Here's a holiday craft that's both easy and fun to make!

Materials you will need
newspaper
a pencil
paper
a bottle of glue
a solid-colored ball ornament
glitter

1. Spread out the newspaper on your work surface. Print the name of the person to whom you are giving the ornament on the piece of paper so you can see how big or small it will need to be to fit on the ornament. If the name is too long, is there a nickname you can use? Or maybe an initial?

2. Once you've got the name the size you want, take the glue bottle and carefully print the name in glue on the ornament, using your paper as a guide. Let the glue set for a minute.

3. Shake glitter over the glue. You may want to pour the glitter into a spoon or measuring cup to sprinkle. Remember, the longer the name, the more glitter you will need. Keep sprinkling until the glue is completely covered with glitter.

4. Place the ornament on the newspaper, glue side up, to dry.

Merry Christmas from Mandie, everyone!

About the Author

LOIS GLADYS LEPPARD has written many novels for young people about Mandie Shaw. She often uses the stories of her mother's childhood in western North Carolina as an inspiration in her writing. Lois Gladys Leppard lives in South Carolina.